Tía Fortuna's New Home

For my granddaughter Mila, I pass this story on to you with all my love.
In memory of Abuela, who made borekas filled with hope.
And to Sephardim everywhere, mazalozo ke sea nuestro avenir.
—R.B.

Thanks always to Jared, Miranda, and Griffin for your love and support.
And to my abuela Chayito, whom I thought of often while painting this story.
—D.H.

THIS IS A BORZOI BOOK PUBLISHED BY ALFRED A. KNOPF

Text copyright © 2022 by Ruth Behar
Cover art and interior illustrations copyright © 2022 by Devon Holzwarth

All rights reserved. Published in the United States by Alfred A. Knopf,
an imprint of Random House Children's Books, a division of Penguin Random House LLC, New York.

Knopf, Borzoi Books, and the colophon are registered trademarks of Penguin Random House LLC.

Visit us on the Web! rhcbooks.com

Educators and librarians, for a variety of teaching tools, visit us at RHTeachersLibrarians.com

Library of Congress Cataloging-in-Publication Data is available upon request.
ISBN 978-0-593-17241-4 (trade) — ISBN 978-0-593-17242-1 (lib. bdg.) — ISBN 978-0-593-17243-8 (ebook) —
ISBN 978-0-593-56806-4 (proprietary edition)

The text of this book is set in 13-point Cabrito Norm Regular.
The illustrations were created using gouache, watercolor,
and colored pencil with digital finishing in Procreate.
Book design by Nicole de las Heras

CIP Code: 0622/B1884/A6

MANUFACTURED IN CHINA
March 2022
10 9 8 7 6 5 4 3 2 1

Tía Fortuna's New Home

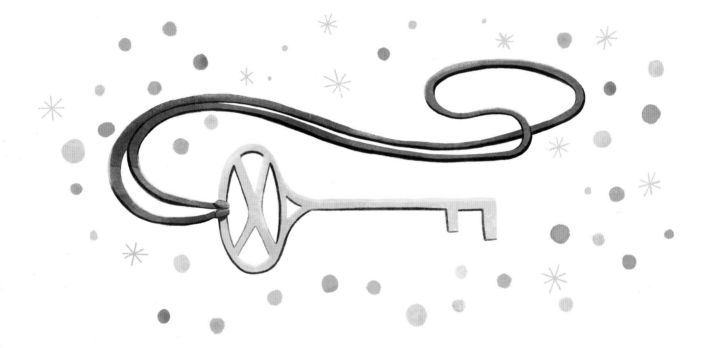

written by

RUTH BEHAR

illustrated by

DEVON HOLZWARTH

Alfred A. Knopf
New York

I love to visit my tía Fortuna in her little pink *casita* at the Seaway.

When my auntie was young, she lived on the other side of the sea, in Havana.

From her rooftop, she waved to the ships as they came into the harbor.

But one day, Tía had to leave, with nothing but a suitcase of old photographs and the mezuzah that hung on her doorpost and a key to a home gone forever.

She felt lost and wept many tears, until she found her *casita* at the Seaway.

She has lived there for years and years.

Today is Tía's last day at the Seaway.

"Why do you have to move, Tía?"

"Bulldozers are coming to tear down the Seaway. A fancy hotel will be built here."

"What will happen to your little pink *casita*?"

"My home will be a memory."

Tía touches the key on her necklace. "Like the home I left in Havana, a memory."

QUE DIOS LE BENDIGA

"But I want to visit you at the Seaway today, and next Friday, and always."

"Estrella, it's time to say goodbye and wish for *mazal bueno*."

Tía gives me a hug, and her lucky-eye bracelets tinkle and twinkle.

"Come, Estrella, *vamos a saludar la playa*—the beach wants to greet you."
We kick off our sandals and breathe in the salty air.

"Look at that bright blue sky! The sun gives everyone its light for free."

el sol, el sol, el sol

"The sea roars all night, and now it's tickling our feet."

el mar, el mar, el mar

Estrella

Tía sinks down into the sand.
"What a pretty *casita* you're making!" she says.

How can Tía be happy on such a sad day?
"Tomorrow the sandcastle will be gone . . . and
so will we!"
"It's not *mañana* yet, Estrella. Let's enjoy today."

When we get back to the Seaway, Tía serves me warm borekas.
"How do you make borekas taste so delicious, Tía?"
"I'll tell you my secret. I fill them with potatoes and cheese and . . . *esperanza*."

"How can borekas be filled with hope?"

"Because they are the food of your grandfathers' grandfathers' grandfathers and your grandmothers' grandmothers' grandmothers. They took them from Spain to Turkey to Cuba. Now we eat them here in Miami."

Tía smiles. "We come from people who found hope wherever they went."
"Esperanza, esperanza, esperanza," I say aloud.
And I help Tía pack a box with the rest of the borekas.

esperanza,
esperanza,
esperanza

"Is that all you're bringing with you?" I ask.

"I don't need much," she replies. "I have so many memories in my suitcase right here," and she points to her head.

Mommy arrives, and she's in a rush.

"Wait!" Tía says. "I need my good-luck mezuzah."

But Tía's mezuzah is so crusted with sea salt, it won't budge.

Finally Tía asks, "Mezuzah, would you please come with me?"
and it pops out.

Tía locks the door and slips the big brass key in her pocket.

"Goodbye, *mis palmeras*, goodbye," she whispers.

Palm trees, swooshing, answer her,

adiós, adiós, adiós

We leave the sea behind and drive toward the
banyan trees and the butterflies.
At the front gate, I feel Tía's hand tremble.
"Tía, where are we?"
"La Casa de los Viejitos," Tía says.

She leans against a banyan tree and runs her hands along its rooty trunk.

"Hello, glad to meet you. You've been here awhile, haven't you?"

The banyan tree nods its head at Tía and says,

hola, hola, hola

We step inside, and Tía says, "Let's share the borekas with everyone we meet."
Soon they're all saying thank you.
"You're welcome!" Tía replies, and makes new friends right away.

The lady next door to Tía's room hears us speaking Spanish.
"I once lived by the port of Havana and waved to the ships,"
she says.
"So did I!" Tía tells her. "I'm glad we'll be neighbors!"
They laugh together like old friends.

Mommy carries in Tía's suitcase.

I help nail the salty mezuzah to the new doorpost.

I arrange Tía's pillows on her bed.

"Here's a good place for your photo albums," I say to Tía.

"*Gracias,* Estrellita. It's starting to feel so cozy already!" Tía says.

She gives me a hug, and her lucky-eye bracelets tinkle and twinkle.

"Tía, next time I visit, we'll sit in the garden and watch the butterflies dance."

"*Mashallah,* God willing," Tía says. "Until then, here's a gift for you, Estrella."

She puts something cool in my palm and squeezes my hand around it—
THE KEY TO THE SEAWAY!

"Look, Tía. I'll carry it with me always!"

And as soon as I slip the big brass key around my neck . . .

I hear the sea laughing and smell the salty air.

I can see the grandmothers and grandfathers from long ago, carrying borekas from Spain to Turkey to Cuba to Miami.

At the front gate, we watch the night spread its blanket over the world.

"Look, Tía. The first star is lighting up the darkness everywhere."

Estrella,
estrella,
estrella

she replies.

Tía gives me a goodbye
hug, and as I turn down the path,
I whisper *"Mazal bueno"*
into the starry night.

Author's Note

This story about Tía Fortuna is a portrait of the life of a Sephardic Jew from Cuba. The word *Sephardic* comes from *Sefarad,* the Hebrew word for Spain. The Sephardim descend from Jews who once lived in Spain and were forced to leave in 1492 because of their religious beliefs. Many took to the sea and found a new home in what is now Turkey. In the last hundred years, most of the Sephardim have moved to the United States, Latin America, and Israel. Some settled in Cuba and fell in love with the tropical island, but after the revolution in 1959, they lost their livelihoods and migrated to Miami, starting over once again.

Sephardic Jews never forgot their Spanish ancestry. Elders remain who speak the ancient Spanish from when they lived in Spain centuries ago, a language known as Ladino, or Judeo-Spanish, carried through many migrations. It is a melodic Spanish, sweet to the ears.

A common belief among Sephardic Jews is that they can be hurt by the evil eye. They think that if things are going too well, they might be jinxed. To protect themselves, they wear good-luck charms, like Tía Fortuna's colorful bracelets with the little eyes. And they eat borekas, pastries stuffed with delicious things like mashed potatoes and cheese. They are the food of a people who have moved from shore to shore throughout their history. The legend says that the Sephardim carried the keys of the homes they lost wherever they went, and that gave them hope for the journey ahead.

I am a child of two Jewish civilizations—Ashkenazi on my mother's side, inheriting powerful Yiddish traditions, and Sephardic on my father's side. Since I was closer to my mother's family, the Sephardic traditions seemed more mysterious, and also more magical. Like Estrella, I picked up bits and pieces of a Sephardic heritage and was fascinated by the resilience of the culture that was being passed on to me.

Although Tía Fortuna and Estrella are fictional characters, I am lucky enough to have a lovely, real-life Sephardic aunt who lives in Miami Beach and serves me borekas whenever I visit. The Seaway is a real building, too. I used to dream of living there, and I was very sad to hear of plans to tear it down and build a luxury hotel. I was thinking about this news one day when I was visiting my aunt, worrying that our Sephardic traditions might be lost. I wanted to be a child again, like Estrella, and be assured that my history would be kept alive.

Many efforts are being made to revitalize Sephardic music, cooking, and literature, and even Ladino as a language. But most important, we must keep on telling the stories and passing them on. People of Sephardic heritage need to hear these stories to find out who they are, but so do all who wish to take part in the beautiful diversity that is the soul of our humanity.

Glossary

All words and phrases listed here are Spanish unless otherwise marked.

a dank—thank you (Yiddish)

adiós—goodbye

arigato—thank you (Japanese)

boreka (also spelled *bureka* or *boureka,* or *börek* in Turkish)—turnover, pastry pie, empañada

casita—little house

el mar—the sea

el sol—the sun

esperanza—hope

Estrella—a common Sephardic name, meaning *star* in Spanish (pronounced ess-TREH-yah)

gracias—thank you

hola—hello

la Casa de los Viejitos—Home for the Aged

mañana—tomorrow

mashallah—God willing (Arabic), an expression widely used by Sephardic Jews

mazal bueno—good luck (Hebrew and Spanish), a Sephardic blessing

merci—thank you (French)

mezuzah—a small box containing a parchment scroll with the *Shema* prayer, placed on the right doorpost of Jewish homes to protect those who live inside (Hebrew)

mis palmeras—my palm trees

obrigado—thank you (Portuguese)

shukraan—thank you (Arabic)

todah—thank you (Hebrew)

vamos a saludar la playa—let's go say hello to the beach

Thank You

With gratitude and love to Alyssa Eisner Henkin, Nancy Paulsen, Ann Pearlman, Richard Blanco, Marjorie Agosín, Margarita Engle, Karen Greenberg, and my generous teacher Sandra Cisneros, who showed me how to make the story sing. *Cariños* to my husband, David; my son, Gabriel, daughter-in-law, Sasha, and granddaughter, Mila; Tía Fanny; and Mami and Papi.

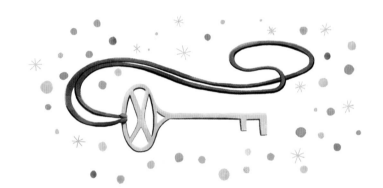